A Heart with Many Rooms

J.W. James

Published by FemDomLit Publications, 2024.

A HEART WITH MANY ROOMS

First edition. December 14, 2024.

Copyright © 2024 J.W. James.

ISBN: 979-8230406310

Written by J.W. James.

Also by J.W. James

Women Rule. Men Obey
Going Down on Her Lover
A Heart with Many Rooms

Cover art provided through pexels.com. Photo by Marlon Alves

This is a work of erotic romance fiction. It is designed to excite the mind and body, and easily-offended readers are urged to use caution when selecting this work. All sexual activity contained herein is consensual and involves only adults, eighteen years and older. This work concerns a woman-led relationship, in which a strong man surrenders to the leadership of a stronger woman. Such relationships are sometimes referred to as Female Domination (FemDom), Female Led Relationships (FLR), or Gynarchy/Matriarchy. It is the view of all who are connected with this work that such relationships are a natural expression of love and affection for a significant portion of the population but is neither "the way things really are" nor "the ways things should be" unless people choose this path as a means of finding love, devotion, and giving purpose to their lives. We believe love is love; and support the right of all adults to enter freely into whatever loving relationship fits their needs.

Can you do me a favor?

JUST LET US KNOW WHAT you think. Seriously. That's all we're asking for. When you leave a review/rating, you do two things. You let us know where we get it right and where we don't. That's important because we will keep missing the target unless you let us know where it is. Help us help you.

The other thing is that it tells retailers that someone out there believes this book is worth reading. That's important because retailers automatically move books higher in searches based on their reviews/ratings. Having no reviews and no ratings leaves us trying to be the prettiest drop of water in the ocean. Telling retailers what you think of us not only helps them make better suggestions for you, it helps everyone else wade through the thousands of pages of results to find something they like.

And it helps us sell more books. Let's be honest – we are in business to sell books. If we can't sell books, we can't pay our bills, and that means we have to stop writing. No one wants that (we hope).

Thank you, and we hope you enjoy what follows.

Tomio Hall-Black

J.W. James

FetDomLit Publications

1

CODY LAY ON HIS BACK and stared through the darkness at the ceiling. The closet was long enough for him to stretch out in, but it wasn't very wide. Still, he could put his hands behind his head and try to make sense of his life while the sounds of his wife fucking yet another stranger came through the closet door.

Patricia's soft panting marked the tempo of her lover's efforts. The moans and whimpers that were cut short with kisses and bursts of ecstatic glee reminded him of how quiet she had always been with him. The sounds of his wife's pleasure were the result of his failures as her lover.

"Fuck! Yes!" Patricia groaned. "Like that! Like that!"

Inside the metal cage his wife kept locked on it, his cock throbbed and ached to be used. Even if it was only his hand, he wanted something. Anything. But this was Patricia's rule. He was her cuckold, and he was going to be a horny cuckold.

A man's voice growled too low for Cody to make out the words. But he could hear the man's flesh slapping between his wife's legs. Heard her trilling gasps of pleasure as this stranger's cock plowed her the way she'd forbidden him.

"Almost," Patricia said, her voice trembling with building tension. "Don't stop! Don't stop!"

Cody distracted himself by counting how many times this scene had been enacted. Six months ago, Patricia had given him the ultimatum

– life in chastity as a cuckold or divorce. At the time, he had figured the first choice wouldn't last long and it would only be a little private humiliation for his wife to enjoy. She'd taken six guys the first month, and another five the following month. He'd stopped counting. Somewhere between twenty and thirty guys had fucked his wife while he'd listened to it.

"Wait for me!"

His imagination gave him more details than he wanted. Patricia, on her back, arms and legs around someone else. Her body arching, firm breasts rocking with the rhythm of her lover's thrusts. Soft, brown eyes losing focus as pleasure peaked. Full, warm lips parted just enough to pant for breath.

"Almost! Wait! Wait for me!"

"I'm coming!"

The bed rattled against the wall. The man's nasally growls turned guttural, almost animalistic. Then he cried out, and Cody knew this man was pumping cum inside his wife's pussy.

"Yes! Yes!"

He had learned to hear the exact point when Patricia's body gave over to orgasm. There was as specific catch in her breath. A certain way her whimpers hitched. A tell-tale shuddering of her panting breath into hard huffs of air.

Cody's cock ached for freedom. It strove to even lift the cage so it could extend fully. But the hard steel held firm, and his cock was only able to swell against its confines. He knew that, if he looked, it would be pressed between the ribs of the cage. It twitched in frustration, and Cody felt his cock fill with weeping pre-cum. When he wiped his hand at the cage, it came away wet, telling him that he'd been so excited that he'd been leaking for some time.

Patricia laughed. Full-throated and filled with the sheer joy of her existence. Cody always wondered if she laughed like that because the orgasms felt so good or if because she was thinking of her poor, humiliated husband lying in the closet. Regardless, he wanted to be the man that held her when she laughed like that. To feel the way her throat vibrated with happiness as he kissed her there. He wanted to be the one that gave her that happiness. That made her feel that wonderful.

The stranger's laugh joined Patricia's. Cody tried not to think about his hands stroking her sweat-soaked skin. Kissing her breasts and squeezing her ass as his cock softened inside of her. Feeling Patricia's hands stroking his back and shoulders.

"You need a shower," Patricia said.

"I didn't ask." The man laughed, like it was a joke, but there was a serious level of disrespect in his tone. "Maybe I like to have your scent on me. Maybe I like the stench of your pussy."

Silence blossomed, and Cody wished he could somehow peak into the room to see what was happening. Was Patricia glaring at the man? Was she laughing with him? What?

"This is my house," his wife declared, her voice frosty. "And if you want this pussy again, you follow my rules. That means you shut your mouth and take a shower. You stink. Not like pussy, like a sweaty man who hasn't washed his pits. Take a fucking shower or leave."

"I don't really like that tone," the stranger growled. "You're just a piece of ass. Don't start acting like you run me. I can be balls deep in another woman before sundown tomorrow."

"Knuckle deep in your own hand, more like it," Patricia snapped back. "You're just a dick. I don't even remember your name. And your ability to get laid depends on your ability to convince a woman you have something in your pants more noteworthy than what she keeps in her top drawer. All I have to do is show a little cleavage, give a little giggle, shake my ass a little, and I've got any man I want following me home to show me how pathetic you were." She gave a cruel bark of laughter. "I'm a piece of ass? You're just a sack of meat that I don't have to change the batteries in."

There was the sound of clothing sliding over a body. Steps fell heavy down the hallway and the front door slammed shut. A few moments later, a car roared to life and took off down the street. Cody waited until Patricia opened the closet door.

"Come on out, babe," she told him. "I need a shower."

He followed his wife to the bathroom. As she sat on the toilet, Cody adjusted the water temperature. With a soft chuckle, his wife's fingernail found the streak of pre-cum that had leaked down his balls.

"Must have sounded good," she said.

"You sounded good," he told her. "You always sound good."

She gave him a soft smile. He stepped into the shower as she tore off a handful of paper to clean herself.

"I'm sorry he turned out to be an asshole," he said, taking his wife in his arms as she joined him in the shower. "You deserve better than that."

"I have better than that," she replied, lifting her mouth to kiss him. "And I knew exactly what response I'd get when I gave him that order." She shrugged. "Maybe I wanted to fight with him a little, so he didn't want to come back."

His arms wrapped around her, pulling her naked body against his. Her arms encircled his neck, pulling his mouth to hers again and again. When he moaned and filled his hands with her ass, she opened her mouth to suck his tongue against hers.

"I need you, Patricia," he said, hunger resonating in his voice. "God, I love you!"

"I love you, too," she replied, petting the back of his head as his mouth worked on her throat. "You have to trust me. I know what I'm doing."

He groaned his frustration, digging his fingers into the flesh of her bare ass. This was more tortuous than listening to her fuck. His cock fought the chastity cage, but the stainless steel was as impervious to hunger for his wife's flesh as she was.

"You're driving me crazy," he sighed, fighting to control himself. "That's what you're doing. Driving me crazy."

She gave a soft bark of laughter.

"You make yourself crazy. I do what I have to do because I know what we need." She tilted her face into the shower spray. "You can find a way to not let it bother you. You choose not to."

Patricia turned in his arms, handing him the shampoo bottle over her shoulder. He took it, dumped a palmful of the coconut-scented soap, and began massaging it into her wavy honey-blonde hair. She tilted her head one way, then the other. Sighed with contentment.

"This is what I need," she assured him. "This shows me more love than your cock every could."

"I can't help wanting you," he said. "I don't know what you want from me. I can't stop being a man."

She let him rinse the shampoo from her hair. Turning, she kissed him again, before turning her back again. He took the conditioner from her and began to work that into her hair.

"I don't want you to stop being a man," she told him. "I want you hungry for me. I want you horny." She paused and looked over her shoulder at him. "I'm not doing this to hurt you, Cody. You know that."

Turning to face him, she looked up at her husband as she held her body against his. One of her hands rested on his cheek and she lifted on her toes to give him a soft, wet, loving kiss. He gave a soft sigh and rested his face on her shoulder.

"You aren't going to be in the closet forever," she promised. "When I find the right man, everything will be perfect. You'll see. You just have to trust me."

He trusted her. He truly did. If that were not so, then their marriage would have ended six months ago. The problem was that he did not have her vision, and she was reluctant to give him details. She needed a second man, but he didn't understand why.

"I want you to be a man," she assured him. "But I want you to be a man who understands his place and is strong enough to let me have my place, too." She paused, as if thinking. "What I want is for you to realize that you love me enough to let me have what I need from you and take what you can't give me from another man I will love equally."

Cody ran his hands over his wife's body. He hated the idea of sharing her – not that he was actually sharing, since he didn't get what she was giving others. What he wanted was to have her for his own, and never let anyone else touch her. He knew better than to say that, though, because Patricia would never allow him to continue to hold that false hope.

"What if I can't give you that?" he whispered, afraid of her answer.

"Don't be stupid," she said, turning the water off. "You already are."

2

"DO YOU REMEMBER ME mentioning Robert Falstaff?"

Cody looked across the dinner table at his wife. Truthfully, he couldn't remember the names of half the people she talked to him about. Their names didn't seem to be the important part of what she said. He chewed slowly, searching his mind. After half a minute, he shook his head.

"I don't think so," he said.

Patricia's eyes lit up in a way that made his heart race. She chewed her lower lip slowly. He thought a hint of color slid up from her collarbone to her cheeks.

"And old boyfriend?" he asked, and she shook her head.

"No, but almost," she said. "Back in high school, we kind of hand a mutual crush. But Jenny Taylor also had a crush on him and Robert's best friend, Stan, had a crush on me. I ended up dating Stan and he ended up dating Jenny, and even when we broke up, we couldn't really date our best friend's ex, you know?"

He didn't know that, but he took it as a rule in her life. At least, when she was a teenager. Now? He wasn't sure if she had any rules. Well, for her. She had plenty of rules for him.

"Anyway, I saw Robert at the grocery store this evening after work," Patricia continued. "He moved away after school, but he just moved back about three weeks ago. Can you believe it?"

10

Cody didn't like the direction this was headed, but he kept his fears to himself. It was easier to enjoy his wife's enthusiasm. As she spoke, she radiated happiness. She laughed and smiled at him, and he fell in love with the woman across the table from him all over again.

"You're beautiful," he told her.

"Um, thank you," she said, giggling. "You understand what I'm leading up to, don't you?" When he didn't answer, she said, "Please, don't take my joy. Try to be happy that I get a second chance at a guy I always wanted to be with."

"If he makes you happy, then I'll be happy," he promised. "I'll find a way. I mean, how could I not be happy if you're happy."

Patricia stopped eating and put her fork down. She looked down at her plate.

"I know you're just being honest," she said. "I just..." She closed her eyes and sighed. "I don't want to use him to hurt you. I want you to love this. I want you to want it to work."

He remained silent. If she would only tell him what "it" was, perhaps he could help her make "it" work.

"So, you're going out with him this Friday?"

Meeting her husband's gaze, Patricia shook her head.

"He's going to pick me up in half an hour," she said. "We're going to have a drink or two and see how we feel for each other." After a pause, she added, "I don't want you to wait up for me. Just... take the bed tonight. While I'm away."

Despair hit the depths of Cody's belly. He nodded and looked down at his plate. Pushed a green bean around with his fork.

"But it's Wednesday..."

"Does that really matter? She asked. When he didn't answer, she went on, "I want my first time with Robert to just be for us," she said. "This is a big thing for me. Cody, I learned how to pleasure myself with fantasies of this man." She gave a bark of laughter. "He's the first man that got me... wet."

"I get it," he replied. He sat back in his chair but couldn't bring himself to look at his wife. "You don't have to explain..."

"Cody, if he's the one..."

"The one? What does that mean? Never mind. I don't want to know," he admitted, sniffling back a tear. "I don't want anyone to be the one. I should be the one! Why can't I be the one?"

He had gone too far, and he knew it. The certainty that tonight would be the death of his marriage hit him hard. When his eyes burned, he didn't bother to try to hold the tears back.

"Cody." Patricia came around the table and sat in his lap. She held his face to her throat as he cried. "It's okay. I understand. I do." He put his arms around her waist. "It's like... my heart is a big mansion, and you completely fill the room where you and I live. But there are other rooms, Cody."

"It's only Wednesday," he protested. "You only fuck around on weekends."

"I do not fuck around!" she snapped. "Don't be an asshole, Cody! I could do this and not ever let you know!"

"Sometimes I think it would be better that way," he confessed. "Do you know what it's like to hear you fuck other guys?"

She held his glare. Raised one eyebrow.

"Tell me."

"It fucking sucks!" he cried out. "I fucking hate it, Patricia! I fucking hate it! I'm sorry that I can't make you come! I'd do anything to be the guy you want in your bed! I'm not, and I know it, and I hate it! And I hate me!"

Patricia waited for him to go on. When he didn't, she nodded. Kissed his mouth with tenderness and love.

"I can't make you not hate yourself," she said. "But for five years, I hated myself when I let you use my body without getting what I needed in return. You need to understand that. You need to understand that any woman who loved you less than I do would leave you and not think twice about it."

"Maybe that's what should happen," he snapped. "Then you could be with Robert and be wet for him all the time."

Her hand stroked his cheek softly. As much as he tried to stay mad at her, he couldn't. All he could do is love her and want her.

"Ask for it," she said.

"Ask for what?"

She raised an eyebrow. Waited.

"Don't go see him tonight," he said. "Stay home with me. Please."

Her lips were tender against his. She nuzzled against his face. When she brought her mouth to his ear, he could feel her breath glide against his skin.

"I love you, and I will never abandon you," she whispered. "Don't wait up for me."

As if on cue, a horn came from outside. Without looking back, Patricia stood up and walked out the door, taking her purse with her.

Cody remained at the table, staring at the door his wife had walked out of. Other rooms? What the hell did that mean? He would fill up one room and "the one" would fill up all the others? Or would there be other "the one" guys? He just didn't know.

He sat at the table for a very long time, hating everything. He hated his wife. He hated his life. And, most of all, he hated himself. When he was too tired to hate any longer, he cleared off the dishes and put them in the dishwasher. Then he took a shower and climbed into bed.

And, because he could do nothing else, he waited for Patricia to return.

And he waited.

And he waited.

It was almost two-thirty when Cody heard a car door slam in the driveway. A minute later, he heard his wife come in and lock the door behind her. Her shoes clicked softly on the hallway floor.

"Hey," she said, her voice soft. Her face broke into a happy smile when she saw him. "I told you not to wait up for me."

"I couldn't help it," he said, shrugging. His lips sucked at hers when she stretched out on top of him. "I love you," he whispered. "I'm sorry."

Patricia shook her head twice and lifted away to look at her husband. She smiled and kissed him again.

"Don't ever be sorry for wanting me," she said. "It's okay to want to be greedy."

His hands moved down her body until they cupped her butt. She opened her mouth to him, sucking his tongue against hers. His hips pushed up at her.

"Ask me," she whispered between kisses. "Ask me if I fucked him."

"I don't care—"

"Ask!"

Cody's voice failed him, but his wife waited. She petted and kissed him, showing him that it was okay to struggle with this. He had to bury his face in her shoulder, hiding from her gaze.

"Did you fuck him?"

"No." When he gave a muffled sob, she cradled him in her arms. "But not because of you, Cody. It just wasn't the right time for us."

"Let me be with you tonight," he whispered against her neck. "Unlock me. Let me be your husband. I need you."

"I'm here, my love," she replied. "But you're going to stay locked and hungry." He began to continue his protests, let them devolve into outright begging but she placed a fingertip to his lips and shook her head. "Don't ask again. Accept it."

She waited until he nodded. With a kiss, she moved away from him and began to undress. His hungry eyes devoured her as she did so.

"I'm not trying to rub your nose in anything," she said, shrugging off her bra. "But I want to tell you about my night." She slid an oversized shirt over her head before stepping out of her underwear. "Because it was a very different night than I expected."

Patricia left the lamp on her nightstand on when she slid under the covers. Her soft, warm body pressed against Cody's and his cock throbbed its awareness to him. If his wife noticed, she gave no clue.

"Robert is back in town because his mother died two months ago," she said, snuggling against Cody's chest. "A few months before that, he finalized a rather bitter divorce that resulted in very limited visitation with his teenage son. He had to find a new place to live, and his mother's house is close enough to work and to his son, so he is fixing it up."

"Sounds like he's having a rough year," Cody said.

"He is," Patricia agreed. "But he's a good guy. Strong. Holding up pretty well." She sighed. "His mother's house has this big, screened porch, and it has this big swing on it. So, we sat there together and just talked." She shrugged. "We may have kissed a few times."

"I would think him stupid if that weren't true."

Laughing, Patricia kissed her husband.

"I told him about us," she said. "About our... arrangement. What I want. How you struggle with it." A heavy sigh fell against his chest. "I don't know how or why we got to it, but he was very easy to talk to. And... I guess I kind of wanted him to know. I mean, if it works with him and me, then..."

She ended with a shrug.

"Then you won't need me?"

Patricia sighed heavily.

"You know I don't mean that," she said. "You're my husband. I love you. That's it. Period."

"Not quite."

Another sigh, and she said, "Okay, there's more to it than that. But what I'm saying is that you and I are a team, unless you decide you need to move on." She brought her mouth to his quickly. "And before you say it, I don't want you to move on. I want you here. With me."

"And him."

"Maybe." Silence fell between them. She petted his cheek and kissed him again. "It can work, Cody. I know it can. Trust me."

"I'm trying." He stroked his hand down her back. His cock ached to be inside of her. It wasn't just physical, though. He needed that intimacy, the closeness that came from bodies merging into one. "So, the whole many rooms thing. Is it like, I have a room and I'm not allowed out of it? You just come and visit me?"

"You're being stupid," she said with a yawn. "I'm with you now. Accept it."

Cody held his wife until her breathing became slow and even. He knew he wouldn't sleep tonight. He'd have to call out from work tomorrow. There's no way he could work after being awake and worrying about his wife loving another man. And no matter how hard he tried he couldn't see it being any other way. And he couldn't see it working the way Patricia seemed to think it would.

3

CODY PARKED THE CAR in front of a small, but tidy craftsman-style home that looked like it dated to the middle part of the previous century. The yard was also small, but tidy, with hedges between the neighboring houses that showed signs of recently being cut back from overgrowing. Beds had been lifted on either side of the porch but remained unplanted.

"He's done a lot of work to bring it back," Patricia said. "It was beautiful when we were kids. His father was an incredible green thumb."

"It's a nice house," Cody agreed. He didn't much care about architecture or homes and gardens, but he could see that a lot of care had been needed to bring the house back to life. "Nice neighborhood."

They got out of the car and Patricia held her hand out to her husband. He took it, letting her lead him up onto the porch and through the screen door. It was decidedly cooler on the porch than the sultry August evening. He could see the porch swing where Patricia said she had kissed Robert and talked with him late into the night. There was something intimate about the porch, maybe because of the screen. It felt warm and inviting.

"I'm so excited!" Patricia said, turning to kiss him. "I love you, Cody! I love you so very much!"

"I love you," he told her.

He was still kissing her when the door opened. Cody stepped back to see a tall, well-muscled man in jeans and a tee shirt smiling at him.

Robert had dark hair that was cut short on the sides and long enough on top that it had to be combed back. A well-groomed beard covered his cheeks. His eyes met Cody's an instant before Patricia stepped into his arms.

Robert had a nice laugh, and he seemed happy to have Cody's wife in his arms. They embraced, and when he looked down, Patricia lifted on her toes to bring her mouth to his. One of her hands moved behind his head to hold him to her kiss, and Cody saw her jaw move when she opened her mouth to take his tongue.

As much as he hated it, his cock began to swell as he watched Patricia kiss the other man. As Robert's hand slid down to cup her ass, his cock found the limits of its confines but continued to try to grow. It pressed against the cage until it ached from it. Patricia's very feminine moan of pleasure brought it to its full length, and he was sure it would start dripping soon as Robert's other hand grabbed her ass.

Patricia stepped back, disentangling her arms from Robert's, to stand next to her husband. With a giggle, she turned and kissed Cody as passionately as she had Robert. Surprised, Cody took a moment before he kissed her back. When she pulled her mouth from his, he was nearly breathless.

"Cody, this is Robert," she said, grinning like a Cheshire cat. "Robert, this is my husband, Cody."

"Pleased to meet you," Robert said, holding out his hand. As Cody shook it, he added, "Patricia has told me some quite remarkable things about you." He waved a hand and stood aside. "Come on in. I just threw some steaks on the grill in back."

They followed him through the house, Patricia pulling slightly ahead of her husband. Pushing into the backyard, Cody was surprised to find a wide expanse of concrete with a metal roof over it. A modern outdoor kitchen was built along one side, with a round picnic table in the center. Comfortable-looking deck chairs were scattered about. It all looked new, so he guessed that Robert really had put some effort into fixing up his childhood home.

"Pick a seat," Robert called over his shoulder. He opened a small fridge under the prep counter. "Beer? Wine?"

"Cody likes beer," Patricia answered. "I know we're having steak, but will anyone be offended if I ask for a white wine?"

Robert looked around at the empty patio. He pulled a bottle of wine from the fridge and showed it to a crowd that wasn't there.

"Any protests?" he asked. "No? Then the lady gets to drink what she wants."

He poured a healthy amount into a wine glass and handed it to Patricia. Then he pulled two beers from the fridge.

"I don't usually drink beer from a glass," he said. "Bottles okay with you?" When Cody shrugged, he twisted the top off one and handed it to him. Then he opened the other and held it for a toast. "Good food and good friends."

"Good times," Patricia said, clinking her glass to his bottle.

"Good... uh..." Cody clinked his bottle. Nothing came to mind. "God?"

Robert threw back his head and laughed. Patricia gave him a small smile that few wider until she was also laughing. Unable to resist, even though he didn't get the joke, Cody joined the laughter and drank. Patricia leaned into him, laying a hand against one of his cheeks as she kissed him.

"I love you," she whispered. "This is going to work. I feel it."

"Hey, lovebirds, you need a room?" Robert laughed as he flipped the steaks. "I have some bakers in the oven and a salad in the fridge. Do we need anything else?"

"Sounds good," Patricia said. "I'll get the stuff from inside. You boys can hang out and relax."

She gave Cody a kiss before she stood. Walking over to Robert, she laid a hand on his shoulder. When he turned, she kissed him, too. Robert watched her backside sway as she walked into the kitchen.

"That's an amazing woman," he said. He looked over at Cody for a second before he took a seat close to him. Leaning his elbows on his knees, he lowered his voice. "Man to man, I'm not sure how I feel about this." He pointed between the two of them and then at Patricia. "It sounds good, the way she explains it, but..." Shaking his head, he sat back and took a drink of beer. "I had a hell of a time with a marriage that only included one person. And it didn't work. I don't know about this."

"Patricia told me about your marriage," Cody said. "I'm sorry."

"Thanks." Blue eyes fastened on Cody. "Look. If it's the only way I get a chance to be with Patty, I'll try it. But you and me? We have to be straight. All the way. If there's anything not right for you, you have to let me know. Not her. She'll want to work it out. If it isn't right, I'll step back. It has to be like that. You feel me?"

Cody blinked. No one called her Patty. That was one of the first rules she'd laid down when they were dating. Her name was Patricia. Cody took a swallow of beer. There was a surge of emotion that he wasn't prepared for. He had wanted to hate Robert, and here he was acting like a real stand-up kind of guy.

"I'll let you know," Cody assured him. "All that really matters is that Patricia's happy, I guess."

"That's bullshit, bro." He swigged his beer. "I need to be happy. You need to be happy. We all need to be happy with each other. Otherwise, it's just people fucking with other people's hearts, and I divorced a woman for that."

Unable to find any reply, Cody held out his beer. Robert gave half a grin and tapped his bottle. They drank together.

Patricia came out the backdoor with a large bowl in one hand and a serving tray in the others. He watched his wife set the food on the picnic table. His eyes roamed from her mouth to her throat down to her breasts.

When she turned her back to him and leaned over the picnic table, he stared hard at her ass. God, he wanted her!

As if she could feel her husband's eyes, she looked over her shoulder and caught him staring. She gave him a sultry grin and wiggled her butt slowly. His cock again expanded to fill the cage that held it, not quite fully hard but enough to make it ache.

In the first few weeks of wearing a cage, he had hated that feeling. Dreaded it. He had no idea if the cage made his erections last longer, but he was all too aware of each second that passed while he was hard and caged. If he became full hard, it not only was constricted along the entire length of it, but it fought to lift the heavy piece of metal. Although it was hinged, it did not move nearly enough to provide him with any sense of relief. It was like trying to bend his hard dick in the morning so he could piss, but it didn't stop. He'd thought of it three kinds of torture – too narrow, too heavy, and, of course, it kept him horny.

Complaining to Patricia hadn't gotten him the response he'd wanted. He'd wanted to be taken out of the cage. He wanted her hands or mouth – he understood she wasn't going to let him have her pussy – on his cock. He wanted to come. Instead, she'd given him the first of many wicked grins and teased him, having him beg to be released so she could turn him down again and again.

If his cock got no harder than what it was, it would be okay. He had come to like the slight reminder of his imprisonment that a partial erection brought. It was manageable. Then Patricia gave him that wicked grin and he knew she was going to make him ache for her.

Standing straight, she pulled her long honey-brown hair back from her shoulders to expose her neck. She tilted her chin and ran her fingers down the length of her throat, her eyes telling him that she remembered how much his mouth loved to taste her there while he was in her. His cock remembered, and it swelled again. Not quite all the way, but he could feel it squeezing against its metal prison.

Patricia turned away from her husband, giving her hips a little extra sway as she walked over to Robert. She slid her arm around the man's waist and bumped his hip with hers. His arm snaked over hers, pulling her against him. When he looked down and smiled at her, she lifted on her toes, her lips parting as her other hand cupped the back of his head. Robert turned his face just enough for their noses to miss, his tongue already pushing between Patricia's open lips.

Now Cody was fully hard. So hard that it almost took his breath away. He watched as their lips drew apart and Patricia offered her throat. Somehow his cock grew even harder as Patricia closed her eyes in pleasure, as Robert's mouth tasted her throat the way he had in the shower a few days ago. He watched Robert's hand slid down to squeeze her ass.

His wife opened her eyes to stare at him, challenging him to stop her. All he did was take another sip of his beer. He had to admit, they made a sexy couple. Half of him hoped she would follow through on her threats of making him watch her with someone else. Somehow, watching this man fuck his wife didn't sound nearly as horrible as it had the first time Patricia had teased him about being with someone else. Maybe they would even do it right now. Before dinner.

Robert drew back and looked in Patricia's eyes. She laughed, and Cody could see even from his distance that her eyes were dancing. She kissed Robert again, then walked back to her husband. She leaned over in front of him, knowing her breasts would pull her shirt open and he would look down at the beautiful swell of her flesh.

"I'm so fucking wet right now," she whispered to him. "Are you hard for me, lover?"

"You know I am," he whispered back. It made her giggle. He had to take another swallow of beer to say, "You two look good together. Like..."

His words petered out. He didn't know how to quantify how pleasant it had been to see her with Robert. Truth be told, he wasn't sure why he felt that way. As soon as he told himself that lie, he knew it for what it was.

"He makes you happy," he said.

It wasn't a question, but Patricia grinned and nodded.

"He does," she said. "Feeling jealous?"

He did. A bit. But jealousy didn't make a man get hard. Cody took another sip of beer.

"I guess," he said and shrugged. "But... I like the happiness in your eyes right now." He couldn't hide the sadness that came to his voice when he added, "I wish I could make you that happy."

"You are," she assured him. "I don't know why I want you here – it isn't to make you jealous or to provoke you." She shrugged. "I'd enjoy being here with him no matter what. Having you here makes it a lot better."

"I want you," he replied. "I would do anything to be your lover again."

She pressed her lips to his. Gentle and tender, the kiss was as chaste as the one she'd given Robert had been passionate.

"You're still my lover. You're just caged." She rubbed her nose against his. "What you mean is that you want to fuck me."

It was. He leaned in and kissed her. When she didn't back away, he held his hand to her breast and squeezed. She tilted her chin and let him kiss her throat.

"I want him to fuck me," she whispered. "I want you to watch. I want you to lick me clean after he comes inside me."

He groaned. He'd licked her clean several times. Like being caged, it was a special kind of torture when he first did it. But he found himself looking forward to cleaning her after Robert. That was new, and he told her that.

"See? You love what I'm turning you into," she whispered. She stood, grabbing his hand and pulling him to the table. "Let's eat. I'm starving!"

Cody sat. The food was good, and Patricia was just as good at keeping the conversation flowing. Surprising himself, Cody found himself enjoying the evening. He helped Patricia carry the dishes back into the house and put them in the dishwasher as Robert cleaned his grill.

"Do you want me to leave you with him?" Cody asked, his heart pounding. He wasn't sure which way he wanted her to answer that. "I can pick you up in the morning, if you like." He watched her eyes glimmer with joy, and he was glad that he had suggested it. "I can clean you up when we get home."

Patricia leaned a hip against the counter and looked out the window over the sink at Robert. Her smile never faded. She gave one long blink and turned to face her husband.

"I want to stay," she said. "But this is different than what I've been doing. I've stayed away overnight before but..." She looked down and twisted the wedding ring on her finger. "This is the first time that my heart wants to stay as much as my body. If I stay... Well, if I stay things won't be the same ever again."

"I'm not really crazy about the way things are right now," he said truthfully, making her giggle. "If you don't stay, you're still going to want him and I'm still not going to be your..." He paused because he'd almost said "lover." Instead, he said, "Sex partner."

"That's true," she said, looking up to meet his eyes again. "But what if I fall in love with him?"

He shrugged. Took her hands in his and kissed the tip of her nose.

"You already are," he said. "And it's okay. Because you're still in love with me, aren't you?" When she nodded, he took her in his arms. He remembered the words she'd used to explain things to him. They fit. "This isn't my room in your heart. It's his." He felt her ball her hands in his shirt. "I love you, Patricia. If I learned anything since you locked me, it's that nothing will change that. Ever."

"You should say good-bye to him," she said, her voice soft. "He's a good man, Cody."

"He had better be," he said. "If I have to share you with him, he's going to have to be the best."

Cody walked back outside to where Robert was wiping down his grilling tools. Their eyes met and Cody gave him the best authentic smile he could. He held his hand out.

"I'm going to take off," he said. "I think you and Patricia need some time alone."

Robert didn't let go of his hand. Turning to face Cody, he searched his face intently.

"I meant what I said." His voice was low and earnest. "If it isn't right for you—"

"It is." He squeezed Robert's hand firmly and held his gaze. "Give her the best you have. She's worth it."

"Yes, she is."

When Robert released his hand, Cody turned and walked around the side of the house. He got in his car, started the engine, and drove away. With no regrets, he didn't look back.

4

THE DOWNSIDE TO HAVING multiple bathrooms, Cody decided, was that there were multiple bathrooms to clean. After he scrubbed the bathtub, the tiles, the toilet and the sink, he was only halfway done. And it just seemed wrong to clean one bathroom and leave the other one dirty. After collecting his cleaning supplies, he went to the smaller bathroom off the bedroom. He checked his watch. It was nine-thirty.

Cody found that the scrubbing was almost a meditation for him. He could blank his mind and not think about his wife and Robert. He didn't worry about why it was so late, and he hadn't heard from her. He just existed, scrubbing and rinsing and polishing.

The temptation was there. He would take out his phone, knowing good and well that he hadn't received a call or message, and check the lock screen. Sometimes he opened it up and made sure that the message notification at the top of the screen hadn't somehow missed notifying him of a message.

"Stupid," he told himself. "Just let it be. You wanted them to have time. So, let them have time."

When he was done with the bathrooms, he stripped the sheets off the bed and put them in the washer. Taking clean sheets out of the closet, he spread them and tucked them at the foot of the bed. His phone told him it was ten-oh-five when he spread the comforter over the bed. He had time to vacuum before he had to run downstairs and put the sheets in the dryer.

"I should do something outside," he said. He fixed a cup of coffee and warmed it in the microwave. "Nice weather won't hold long."

After the front yard was mowed and edged and he'd trimmed around the trees, he moved on to the back yard. By the time he finished that, it was eleven-fifty. Time for lunch.

He grilled a ham and cheese and pulled a cold beer from the fridge. Now that the yard was nice, he decided to sit outside and eat lunch in the back yard. It felt good to sit and let the sun warm his face while the wind tugged at his hair. It would have been better if Patricia were here to share it with. He took out his phone.

One-seventeen.

With a sigh, he took his plate and empty bottle of beer back to inside. While he was there, he loaded the dishwasher. He checked the sheets in the dryer and found them still damp, so he started the dryer for another half hour. Then he brought down a load of Patricia's work clothes and put them in the wash.

Back upstairs, he busied himself with wiping the counters and the cooktop. He swept and mopped the floor. Wiped down the kitchen table. It was two-forty now, and he was running out of steam. His body ached from the constant drive of the day. He wanted very badly to lay down and take a nap, but he knew that he'd only fret about Patricia if he did that.

After folding the sheets and moving Patricia's clothes to the dryer, Robert went back outside. He dug through the garage and found the supplies to wash the cars. The water from the hose was cold, but the day was getting warmer. An hour later, he was done.

"Where is she?" he asked, sitting on the front stairs.

His fear, he finally admitted to himself, was that Patricia would like Robert more than she liked being with the man she was married to. It was easy to believe. Robert was a great guy. He was probably a great guy in bed, too.

Cody made himself consider that. His thoughts wanted to shy away from the topic, but he had to face it. After all the other men his wife had screwed, after all the times he'd heard her coming in ways she never had with him – it was apparent that he was a lousy lay. Maybe Robert could give him some pointers. Because that wasn't pathetic at all.

He peeled off his clothes and took a shower. The water felt as good as the work he'd done today. Cody soaped his body and rinsed. Shampooed. Rinsed. Turning off the water, he stepped out and dried himself. He was just hanging the towel back on the hook when his phone rang. He picked it up and swiped the screen.

"Hey," Patricia said. "Don't cook anything. Robert bought pizza for tonight."

"Pizza's good," he said. "As long as there's no anchovies or pineapple."

"One meat-lovers, one veggie combo," she replied. After a pause, "Thank you for giving me the day with Robert. It was amazing."

Cody smiled. He could hear the joy in her voice. True, it was very much related to what she'd been doing with Robert, but she would not be as happy as she was if he hadn't offered to step back. At least, he'd given her the space to have it. It was almost – almost – worth missing her the whole day.

"You're welcome," he said. "Am I sleeping in the closet tonight? If I am, I want to change the sheets."

There was a pause.

"I haven't decided. Sorry."

As he looked out the window, he saw a black pickup pull into the drive. Robert stepped out of the driver's side and held two pizza boxes aloft as he pushed the door shut with his knee. Patricia bounded out of the other side.

"We're home," she said.

A moment later, Patricia stepped through the door, Robert following. The smell of fresh, hot pizza hit Cody's nose, and he realized he was hungry. As Robert laid the pizza boxes on the table, Cody took out three plates.

"Hi," Patricia said, standing toe-to-toe with him when he turned around. The broad smile and twinkling eyes made his heart happy. "Sorry it's so late. We were... busy."

She slid her arms around Cody's waist and kissed him ever so softly. He started to pull away, but she held him. Her tongue slid against his lips, and when he tried to taste her, she sucked his tongue into her mouth. As her body melded against his, he felt Robert pull the plates from his grasp, and he filled both of his hands with Patricia's firm ass.

Cody drank his wife's kiss like a man from the Sahara drinks water. He pulled into his deepest core, letting it sustain him. Even when his cock throbbed and swelled against his cage, all that mattered was that Patricia's mouth was on his. When she finally pulled back, he was almost breathless.

"You haven't kissed me like that in a long time," he said. "I like it."

"I hope you like more than that," she said. She ran her hands over his shoulders and down his chest. "Cody... I want you."

"Fuck the pizza," he whispered. He was suddenly very aware of how hard his cock was, and he felt his hands tremble. "I need you, Patricia."

She kissed him again. This time he picked her up and sat her on the counter. She wrapped her arms around the back of his neck and moaned into his mouth.

"You're making me wet, Cody," she whispered against his lips.

"Unlock me," he said, his voice husky with desire. "I'll fuck you right here. He can watch."

Patricia smiled at him. That smile told him that she was teasing. He groaned, leaning his forehead against her shoulder.

"That's what I wanted," she said, her eyes dancing. "I wanted my husband to act like he wants to fuck me." She held his cheeks between her palms and kissed him. "You need to eat. I have plans for tonight – and they include you."

Cody's hands were reluctant to leave his wife's ass. He gave it a tight squeeze, lifting her down from the counter. His kiss was fierce, with all the hunger of the last six months fueling it. Patricia squealed with excitement, then wrapped her arms around his neck again and sucked at his tongue as it caressed hers.

"I need you," he panted against her throat when she threw her head back. He could feel her throat vibrate as she hummed approval. "Patricia, please!"

"You need to eat," she murmured. "And I need to eat. I haven't had food all day."

Pulling away, Patricia took three bottles of beer from the fridge. She carried them to the table and took the seat at the end, Robert already seated on her right. Cody sat across from Robert, his stomach growling.

"See?" Patricia said. "You need to eat."

"I've been eating all day," Robert quipped, and Patricia joined him in laughing.

"Okay, you need food. I don't think my pussy is very filling," she said to Robert. Biting into the veggie slice, she moaned. "Is this the best pizza ever or am I just that hungry?"

"It's good," Cody said, eating with gusto. Across from him, Robert did the same. "I take it things went well."

"Things went very well," Robert said, reaching for Patricia's hand as he looked at her. "Your wife is an incredible woman."

"Stop!" Patricia protested with mock humility. Then, sweeping her shoulder-length hair back, she said, "Okay. Keep going. Tell me how wonderful I am!"

"You're the most amazing woman I've ever slept with," Robert told her.

"You're worth having my cock locked up for six months," Cody said, not wanting to be outdone.

A light blush came to Patricia's cheeks. If Cody had meant it as a joke, none of them laughed. Patricia's eyebrows lifted as she looked from Cody to Robert and back. Cody couldn't tell if he'd said the wrong thing or if she was basking in the attention from the both of them. Maybe she was waiting to see if Robert could one-up that. Cody didn't think he could. It was a damn good sacrifice.

"When I heard that you were locked up while Patty... shopped around," Robert lifted her hand and kissed it, looking at Patricia while speaking to Cody. "I thought you were crazy. Why would any man let himself be treated that way."

"She didn't mistreat me," Cody said, feeling the need to defend his wife.

"I didn't mean it that way," Robert apologized. "I mean... well, I didn't understand it. But now, I think I do.

"You do?" Patricia tilted her head as she looked at him. "Am I hearing in there somewhere that I can lock you up, too?"

For some reason, Cody's mouth went dry. His heart hammered. Anticipation slid a tentacle through his guts. He heard the playfulness in his wife's words, but he knew how much truth came out in jest. In what both of them said. There was an anticipation of something longer than a quick fling. He had known in his gut that Robert was not going to be a one-weekend lay. Was he anxious or excited? He couldn't tell.

"Yes," Robert said. "If that's what you need from me. How can I give you anything less than Cody has?"

"Cody is my husband," she pointed out. "We've only spent a night and a day together."

Robert lifted a slice of pizza and bit into it. Chewing gave him time to think, and all three of them knew that's what he was doing. Stalling. Cody took a bite and waited.

"It was only a night and a day," Robert agreed after he'd swallowed and taken a long pull on his beer. "But it was a night and a day I've looked forward to since I learned why my dick got hard."

Patricia leaned over to kiss him, and Robert met her halfway. It wasn't a sexy kiss, but it was passionate. More like a slow burn than a melting heat. When their lips parted, their eyes continued to make love to each other. Cody understood that there was something deep between the two of them, something real. But not, he realized, something that would threaten him.

"So," Patricia said, sitting back in her chair. "I thought it would be a few weeks before we talked about something long term."

"Not long term," Cody said around a mouthful of pizza. "Permanent."

He looked up to see Robert's eyes watching him. A small nod was the man's only response, but Cody could see a lot of pain there. And wariness. If it had been a woman who looked at him like that, he would have taken her in his arms. But Robert was a full-grown man, and Cody wasn't sure how to react.

"I think we should wait for that discussion," Robert said, his voice hoarse with emotion. "I want to have it, but I think I want it too much to do it now."

"That makes no sense," Patricia said with a shake of her head. "If it needs to wait, that's fine. But how can you want something too much."

"Right now, he'll agree to anything you say," Cody offered. Robert gave him wary eyes, but he continued. "He needs to be loved, probably has needed it for a long time. It's like car shopping, if you find a deal that's too good, you walk away. If it's a good deal in a week, then you know it's real. If you change your mind, then you've saved yourself from signing a bad loan."

Robert nodded.

"Thank you for understanding," he said. "I was married for ten years, but the last six have left me so incredibly lonely." He looked down at his hands. "This was the first time since my son was born that I've had sex."

"What?"

Cody looked askance at his wife's outburst.

"I've gone six months," he said. "And if you don't follow through tonight, then who knows how much longer?"

Patricia stared at him, open-mouthed. She sat back in her chair.

"Okay, first, our arrangement is totally different than what he was doing with his wife. Second, his son is seven years old, Cody. Seven years." She shook her head, crossing her arms in front of her. "I don't like the comparison. It makes me feel like you think I'm a total bitch for locking you up. I had my reasons, Cody!"

"I don't think you're a bitch," Cody said, shaking his head. "I've never said that. Okay, not for five and a half months. But... it isn't the sex that makes him vulnerable. I hate to say it, but I could do seven years like this – because I'm not lonely. You make it very clear that you haven't forgotten me. You've just put me on the shelf for a specific period of time.

"Alone and lonely aren't the same thing," Robert said. "I was hardly ever alone. She insisted that we go to dinner parties and be seen about town as a happy couple. She just didn't want to have sex with me." He shrugged. "She wouldn't even let me hold her. Not even touch her when we were in bed." Robert paused and looked at the finger where a wedding band had been. "She wanted to have me, but she didn't want to be with me. I was never alone, but I was always lonely."

"Is that how I made you feel?" she asked Cody. "Be honest. If I've hurt you—"

"Never," he answered, shaking his head. "I was alone in the closet each time you brought a man home, but it wasn't lonely." He shrugged. "Every time you sent someone else away, you brought me back to your bed. You didn't give me sex, but you made me feel loved. Wanted. You made me a part of everything you did." He looked across the table again. "That's what you missed."

"Yeah," Robert said. He took a long pull from his beer. Looking up at Patricia, he told her, "That's why I understand this thing between the two of you. I could do it. If she had wanted other guys, I would have found a way to deal with it. Because I wanted her to be happy. But she didn't want that, because she didn't want me." He lifted Patricia's hand and kissed it.

"I've never felt wanted by anyone the way I felt last night when I was with you for the first time."

"What about now?" she asked. "I mean, it's only a few hours, but is it gone?"

"I still feel that way," he answered. "I see it in your eyes. You want me here. Yeah, you had a vague idea that another guy would be... I don't know, fun. But right now, you don't want another guy. You want me. And I like the way that feels."

She went to him. Pushing between him and the table, she sat on his lap and wrapped her arms around his neck. When she looked down at him, there was something so real and beautiful that passed between them that it nearly made Cody look away in embarrassment.

"I want you," she told him. "I want you, Robert Kirkpatrick, right here in my house." She put her hand over her breast. "I want you in my heart." Her hand lifted to rake her fingers through his hair. "And I want you in my bed. Not just tonight, either. If we have to wait to talk about that, then we'll just enjoy tonight. But I want you to know that conversation is coming, because you are the one I want."

Patricia kissed Robert, soft and sweet and gentle. When she lifted her mouth from his, Cody heard Robert sniffle. At least, he thought, he wasn't the only one overcome with this moment. His wife turned her eyes to him.

"I meant what I said, Cody. I want you. I want to be with you." She sighed. "I've missed making love to my husband."

Cody stood and went to his wife. He bent to press his lips to her shoulder.

"Sometimes you have to give up what you want to get what you need," he said to her. "Right now, Robert needs you to not let this moment pass."

"How do you know?" The question was soft, inquisitive and not demanding in the least. She squinted a little, trying to understand. "How can you know what he needs from me?"

"It's how I would feel," Cody said. "I'll go with you. I'll be with you. But he needs you now."

Patricia looked from her husband to the man holding her.

"Is that what you need? Right now?"

When he nodded, she kissed each of his eyelids. Standing, she led Robert towards the bedroom. Cody watched them go, not quite sure what he was feeling. He wanted to be with his wife. But for a reason he couldn't explain, it was more important to him the Robert be with her. Because he needed her, and Cody only wanted her.

After he put away the pizza, Cody put the dishes in the dishwasher, wiped down the table, and turned off the light. He stood in the darkness for a moment. There had been times in his life when things had changed suddenly, and in big ways. All too often, he hadn't seen them coming. Hadn't been prepared for them. But this moment, he felt. Whatever happened when he walked out of the kitchen and into the bedroom, it would change everything he thought he knew about his life.

But he was ready for it. And that, he realized, was what the last six months had been about. Getting him ready for when she was ready. Making him strong enough to guide them all to whatever awaited.

Cody stopped in the doorway, looking at his wife and her lover in the dim light of the lamp on her nightstand. Patricia lay on her back, Robert between her thighs. With eyes only for each other, she sighed as he filled her again. The corners of her mouth lifted in a wordless declaration of love. If they knew he was present, they didn't give any indication of it.

"I want you, Robert," she said, her soft voice carrying to Cody's ear. "I want you here. I want my Robert. Right here with me."

Cody was unsure if he should join them yet. And if he did join them, should he get undressed, too? He was sure that there was something passing between the two of them, something that would bind them to each other's hearts forever. Watching as Robert used his body to declare his love for Patricia, Cody decided it was beautiful, and he felt lucky to be present.

The scent of Patricia's musk filled the room, and that made Cody's cock as hungry as seeing her naked. Moving without his conscious decision, his feet carried him closer to get a better angle. He wanted to watch Patricia's face. He wanted to see Robert's face. He wanted to witness their love.

Robert held his body over hers, using his entire body to move his cock inside her. Patricia's breasts pointed in opposite directions; her large, pink nipples erect. Every time Robert moved into her, she gasped a little. Every time he pulled back, she whimpered. With her palms pressed against Robert's chest and her thighs lifted so she could lock her heels under his butt, she was more beautiful than he'd ever seen her.

"It's okay to be scared," she told the man making love to her. "Love is a scary thing. But you're safe here. Safe with me."

Cody expected the big man to thrust harder, faster. To growl and pant and shout his passion to the stars. But he did none of that. His hands found Patricia's, and their fingers intertwined. His taught, muscular body continued to move with almost agonizing slowness. Tenderness. A gentleness born of love and need so deep and consuming that even Cody felt like he was standing on the lip of a bottomless pit.

Perhaps it was intuition. Maybe it was just because he, too, was a man. But Cody understood what was going on with Robert. He remembered the look in Robert's eyes when he'd said he would back off if Cody told him to. Robert needed Patricia, but he needed more than her. He needed to hear that Cody wanted this, too. No, he needed Cody to be part of this.

And Cody was surprised to discover that he wanted this, too. He undressed quietly and climbed into bed to stretch his body next to his wife's, only the steel cage on his cock keeping the full length of his body from touching hers. Robert's eyes flicked to him, then back to Patricia.

"You're safe," Cody said, echoing his wife's words. "I want you here, too, Robert. Here in my bed, in my wife. You. No one else."

Robert stopped moving, remaining within Patricia's body. His eyes took in the naked woman beneath him. They lifted to meet Cody's.

"Tell me this is okay," he whispered. "I need to know now, because I fucking need this so goddamn bad that I will go completely crazy if you take this away from me later."

Cody hesitated before running his fingertips against the short hair on the side of Cody's head. It felt so different to touch a man this way. Drawing closer, he pressed his forehead against Robert's. And because he wasn't brave enough to kiss the man's lips, he gave him a soft kiss on the tip of his nose.

"It's okay," he said. "Really."

Rubbing the back of Robert's neck, Cody stretched out again next to his wife. She made a soft noise, and when he turned his head, she kissed him. Soft. Tender. Sweet.

"Thank you," she told her husband. "This is what I want. With him. With you. With us."

As he kissed her, he was aware that Robert began moving again. Patricia arched, rocking her hips to bring his cock against the perfect spot. But with one hand cupping Robert's cheek, she wrapped her other hand around to hold the back of her husband's head. She opened her mouth to take his tongue, rolling with pleasure from both men. When she pulled her mouth from Cody's she was panting hard.

"Just like that, Robert," she panted. "Don't stop!"

He obeyed her. Cody lowered his mouth to her throat, and he felt the mewling whimper vibrate against his lips. He licked her skin, sucked at her flesh. Nibbled. Ached for her and loved her. Passion spiraled faster, as if Cody had released the floodgates with his presence.

Then Patricia's body grew taut. Her breath caught and held. As Robert continued to move within her, her entire body began to shudder. Harder and faster, the tremors grew until her abdomen convulsed, pulling her up against the man above her. She screamed in ecstasy, her cried muffled Robert's chest.

"More!" She panted as she fell back to the bed. "Don't stop, Robert! Exactly like that!"

Her hungry mouth found Cody's then. She sucked hard, taking his tongue against hers. Cries of pleasure were thrown into his mouth. Panting through her nose, Patricia tightened again. If anything, her body was tighter than before, shivering in anticipation of release.

Patricia shook fast and hard as she came again. As her body pulled in a wave of release from her hips to her shoulders, Cody took his mouth from hers. Her mouth fell open in a soundless scream as her husband put his mouth to her ear.

"Make him ours," he whispered, not sure what that meant. "Take him where he needs to go. Let him see that you need him with me here. Make him our Robert."

Cody's words pushed her on. Her hips lifted, pumping at Robert's. She was slick with sweat now, and it ran from her body in rivulets. Her hair was soaked with it. But Patricia didn't slow down the least. She pushed her body against and around Robert's. Her hands clutched at his shoulders. Savage cries of building hunger tore from her lips. Cody watched as Robert rode her, letting her take all the pleasure she demanded from him.

"Don't you fucking stop!" She nearly screamed. "Don't you fucking stop! Fuck! Fuck! Yes! Fuck-yes-fuck-yes-fuck-yes!"

"Love him," Cody said. "Love him like you love me. Take everything he can offer. Make him yours."

"Me," she panted. "Mine. Robert. Mine!"

"I'm yours," Robert said. "I love you, Patty-girl."

Patricia arched, every muscle of her body squeezing so tight that she shook. It was impossible to breath, and she had no air to scream. The hardest orgasm of all hit her, driving her back into the bed. Her body arched again, slammed down. Shivering as she gasped for breath, she let both men hold her.

"This," she whimpered. "This. This. This."

"I'm here," Cody whispered. He rolled the lovers onto their sides so he could spoon behind his wife. "I'm here, my love."

"Me, too," Robert whispered. His cock throbbed inside of her, aching for its own release. "I'm here. I love you."

"Mine." Patricia nearly sobbed the word. "Both of you. Mine."

It took long minutes of adoration for Patricia to float back into her body as the men kissed her and stroked her and covered her with their adoration. Her pussy hummed with delight and sparkles danced along her thighs and forearms. She laughed, pushing her hips at each man in turn.

"I love this!" she gasped. "I love you! I love you both!"

5

PATRICIA LUXURIATED between the two men. What had started out to be an act of love and comfort for Robert had turned into so much more. Not just with Robert, but with Cody, too. It was if an entity had been created that encompassed all three of them. All three were now an "us." But as wonderful as that was, it didn't liberate her from her biology.

"I have to pee," Patricia said, making both men chuckle. When she found her feet and wobbled, they laughed again. "It isn't funny."

Obviously, they disagreed. They looked at each other when she disappeared into the bathroom.

"Funny."

Cody lifted his head to look towards the bathroom. Robert was now lying on his back, his hard cock still wet from being inside Patricia, and Cody took a few seconds to really appreciate how the man had taken care of his body. He watched as Robert curled one hand around his cock and stroked it slowly.

"Not her," Robert said, his eyes on Cody.

"What then?"

"I've never wanted to kiss a man before."

Neither had Cody. But his mouth grew wet when he focused on Robert's mouth. He blinked. Blinked again. His heart hammered in his throat. But when he tried to lean forward to offer his mouth to Robert, nothing happened. Still, he wished Robert would make good on his suggestion.

"I'm not saying I'm going to kiss you," Robert clarified. "I just really want to."

Butterflies plowing through his stomach, Cody moved closer until the barest of spaces remained between his body and Robert's. He wanted very much to kiss Robert. But he was scared. A kiss was too much. He needed something safe. Cody's ran his eyes down Robert's body where the man's hand stroked his cock.

"Let me," he said, watching Robert's face as curled his fingers around Robert's. Around Robert's fingers; and around his cock.

He felt Robert's body jerk. Cody moved his hand up and down. Feeling another man's hard cock in his fingers for the first time. Robert moved his hand away, letting Cody take over.

"If you don't tell me to continue," Cody said. "I'll stop. If it isn't right."

"It's right," Robert said. "Don't stop."

"By all means, don't stop."

Patricia rejoined them, sliding onto the bed on the other side of Robert from her husband. Encouraged by both reactions, Cody pumped his hand faster. Robert groaned.

"Goddamn, that feels good." Robert wrapped one arm around Patricia and pull her against him. They shared a fierce kiss. "This guy knows how to jerk a cock."

Propping up on his elbow, Cody took the time to watch his hand stroking the other man's cock. It was almost hypnotic. He saw Robert's washboard abs ripped as his body began to gather and tighten. Patricia stroked the man's cheek and kissed him, smiling down at him. Feeling her husband's eyes, she turned to him.

"Ready to be unlocked?"

Cody's mouth went dry. He couldn't speak. All he could do is nod.

"Lay down crossways on the bed," she directed. As he obeyed, she went to her jewelry box and removed the key to his cage. Bringing it with her, she climbed on the bed from the opposite side, her thighs sitting astride Cody's chest. "See where he's had his cock?"

She used her fingers to spread her pussy lips. It wasn't necessary. Her pink pussy was still gaping slightly from the way Robert had fucked her for the last night and day. Not much, but he knew he could put his little finger in the hole easily. He watched as Robert took her hips and pulled her back a little. When her pussy was mere inches from Cody's face, Robert slid his cock into her again.

"God, I love that," she moaned. "Like the show, Cody?

"You're beautiful," Cody answered. He felt her fumble with the locking mechanism. His hands ran over her back to the curve of her hips. When the lock clicked open, his cock lifted the cage away from the ring that held it tight against his balls. As she lifted the cage from his cock, he felt his pulse pound into it. What a relief! "Patricia! That feels so good!"

Her wet mouth took the head of his cock, tongue slathering it with her spit. Cody nearly lost it at that moment. But Patricia giggled and pulled back, her thumb and forefinger moving from the base of his cock to the tip. She made a slurping sound at the tip of his cock. The hand she wrapped around his cock and her hot, wet mouth began to pump up and down in tandem.

Above him, Robert used the same rhythm to keep Patricia moaning in pleasure. Cody found himself holding back, trying to extend this incredible moment between the three of them. After six months, he knew he wouldn't last long. But he wanted it to last as long as possible. Just when he could take no more, Patricia lifted her mouth.

"Spread your legs for me," she told Cody. "Robert, hold them for me."

Her hand pumped his cock far too slowly to let him come. Robert leaned over Patricia and dug his hands behind Cody's knees. Lifting them up and pushing them out, he spread Cody so Patricia could rub one wet fingertip against the puckered hole of his ass. She wiggled it, pressing gently until it was inside him. Cody groaned.

"Let it happen," Patricia said, finger fucking his ass slowly. "Enjoy it."

It felt amazing, in fact. She found his prostate and stroked it slowly, keeping time with the hand pulling at his cock. A second finger pushed in before she put the head of his cock back in her mouth. He could feel how hard she sucked as her fingers worked in his ass.

Cody groaned as she milked him. Thick cream that had waited for months flowed through his cock into her greedy mouth. Patricia moaned her encouragement as she drank his cum, her fingers working faster, squeezing him tighter. In short order, he was panting and whimpering.

"That's what I want to hear," she told him, pausing to swirl her tongue around the head of his cock. "I want to listen to my men enjoy what I do to them."

His legs trembling, Cody tried to come. He felt like he could at any moment, But there was something about the way the fingers worked him that prevented it. Or maybe some trick he didn't know that would let him come while Patricia did that. All he could do was pant and feel his cock get drained. Not that he would complain about that. After six months of nothing, it was an incredible feeling.

Watching Robert's cock slide in and out of his wife's pussy, Cody wondered if Patricia planned to have the man come directly into Cody's mouth. It was only slightly different than licking a man's cum out of her. The idea didn't revolt him, like he thought it would. It thrilled him. It wasn't that he wanted to suck the man's dick, but he wanted to feel that big cock spitting hot cum over his tongue.

"Let it happen," Patricia said, but Cody wasn't sure who she directed her words at. Maybe both of them. "Trust me."

He watched his wife crawl forward until Robert's hard cock pulled free to glisten in front of his face. If he lifted just a bit, it would slide into his mouth. The thought surprised him, but he groaned as Robert released his legs. He lay straight, letting his wife climb down his body while Robert's throbbing cock hovered just above his face.

Again, he had the odd impulse to taste it. He didn't think Patricia would mind, but he didn't know Robert enough to gauge how far the man was willing to go. He thought Robert would go for it, but Cody didn't want to mess up what was happening. It was too... wonderful.

"See what happens when you're such a good boy," Patricia said.

This time, Cody was sure she was talking to him as he watched her angle his rigid cock up between her legs. The slick heat of her body enveloped him slowly, as if testing whether he could take it. It was a close thing. He whimpered.

"God, I'm going to come," he panted. "Let me come, Patricia, please!"

She ignored him. Riding him slowly, she let him feel her pussy clench around him. Let him have what she'd denied him for six long months. It took every bit of self-control for Cody not to grab her and pummel his cock into her for the whole four seconds it would take him to come.

When Patricia lifted from around him, he groaned. She hadn't said she would let him come, of course. But he'd hoped. His wife smiled at him as she turned to face him before taking him within her again. She stretched her body over his, nuzzling his face.

"Was it worth waiting for?" she asked.

"You are," he said. "But I'd rather not wait that long again."

Patricia laughed. She rolled with him, pulling him on top of her. He thrust at her, and she allowed it. Five pumps. Six. He was ready to explode. His wife gently tightened her legs around his thighs, pinning him inside her pussy.

"Trust me," she whispered. She kissed his mouth softly. "Let this happen. For us."

Cody felt the bed shift and understood that Robert was behind him. It wasn't until the man rested his hand on Cody's hip and Patricia stretched her fingertips to spread his ass that he realized what was going to happen.

"It's okay," his wife whispered. "I want this. For us."

She watched his face as Robert positioned his cock. It was difficult not to clench. When he felt the man lean forward, he whimpered in fear and anticipation.

"It's okay," his wife repeated. "Take him inside you. Just like you're inside me."

Robert was as gentle with Cody as he had been with Patricia. His body fought, tightening against his will. Robert waited until the muscles relaxed and pushed forward the tiniest bit.

"He's going to fuck your ass," Patricia said. "Let it happen, Cody. I want this. I've always wanted this."

"Oh, God!" Cody felt the head of Robert's cock push him open and force its way inside him. "God! Fuck! Oh, God!"

The tip of Robert's cock slid in and out of Cody's ass, making it flex repeatedly. As Cody's muscles released, Robert pushed in a little deeper. Cody felt the ridge on the head of Robert's cock catch inside of his ass.

"Let him in," Patricia purred. "All the way, lover. It's the only way you get to stay inside me."

Cody panted and whimpered as Robert rocked his hips. The big cock slowly worked deeper into him. It hurt a bit, but the feeling of bare cock sliding through his asshole was more than compensation. Cody realized that he was whimpering because he wanted more cock in his ass.

Caught between the silky wet pussy squeezing his cock and the throbbing cock invading his ass, Cody couldn't move. He felt Cody's weight shift, letting the cock push full depth into him. When Robert ground his cock into Cody's ass, he forced Cody's cock to grind into Patricia's pussy.

"That's what I want," Patricia said with a sigh. She shoved with her hips to rock both men back. "Look at me, Cody. I want to watch you get taken for the first time."

He let his emotions have his face. The fear. The excitement. The way he needed her. Maybe even needed her to push him to this. Above all, the love he held for her.

"I love you," he whispered. "God, I love you!"

She smiled and petted his face. Curling up, she kissed him. Soft. Tender.

"This," she said. "This is the fantasy I was always afraid to tell you. I was afraid you'd freak out and I'd lose you."

"I'll do anything for you," he gasped, feeling Robert's cock exploring his depths. "I'll suck his cock if you want me to."

"I do," she said. "But right now, I want my husband to come inside of me from getting his ass fucked by my boyfriend."

Robert thrust, pushing Cody's cock into his wife. Both Cody and his wife gasped in pleasure.

"Not my boyfriend," Patricia corrected herself "Our boyfriend. Our lover."

6

ROBERT WAS GENTLE. He let Cody feel the way his cock slid out of his ass, making his hole pop when he pulled the head of it out. Then he made Cody grunt in pleasure as he entered him again, filling him with a single, strong thrust of his cock.

"Okay?" Patricia asked.

"Yes," Cody moaned, his ass flexing at the emptiness Robert left behind. A moment later, his ass was forced open again and Cody moaned again. Each time Robert opened him, there was less resistance. "I want to fuck back at him."

"Not yet," Patricia said. "Let him enjoy this. It's his first time with a man, too."

"Did he know what you wanted?"

A soft smile came to her lips.

"Of course, I couldn't expect him to just fuck your ass at the drop of a hat." She rocked her hips and tightened around him. "I talked about a lot of things with him." Watching his face react to the cock sliding in and out of his ass, she asked, "Do you want to kiss him?"

He looked at her, afraid to say he did. Afraid of what it meant if he gave himself into her fantasy fully.

"It's okay," she told him, pushing her fingers against his jaw. "Kiss him. Let me watch."

Robert's hand rested under his chin; his arm wrapped behind Cody's head. Cody's cock begged him to move just a little so it could come as a man's lips touched his for the first time.

"We don't have to," he whispered to Cody. "If it's too much too soon."

"Kiss me," Cody said, his soft voice firm. He leaned back and wiggled his ass at his new boyfriend. "Fuck my ass and kiss me."

He did. Robert's tongue pushed between Cody's lips as he began to pump at him faster. Cody moaned and leaned back to kiss, trying to shove his ass back as he did so.

"Fuck my ass," he mumbled against Robert's lips. "I want to make you come."

Robert's teeth caught his lower lip. He chuckled as he drew back. One big hand rested in the middle of Cody's back, pushing him down against his wife. Patricia wrapped her arm around his neck as Robert began to thrust harder. Faster.

"I know," Patricia cooed as Robert began to jack-hammer Cody's ass. "I remember what it's like to get fucked the first time. Just let it happen, my love. Let it happen. Let yourself enjoy it."

"God! He's fucking me!" Cody whimpered. Patricia soothed him and petted him. "I love this! I love being fucked!"

"He's fucking your ass," Patricia whispered. She tightened her pussy around him and rocked her hips in time with Robert's thrusts. "I want you to come from it, baby. I want to feel you come inside me from having your ass fucked."

Now Robert was growling. His body slapped against Cody's bare ass, creating a staccato beat. There was no gentleness left. It was pure hunger.

"Give me that asshole, boy," he growled. "I'm going to come in your asshole!"

Cody was climbing too quickly to stop. He ground his cock into his wife. Whimpering as his ass was pummeled, he stared down at her. She smiled at him.

"Let it happen," she said for what had to be the hundredth time. "When it's time, you won't be able to stop it."

Robert roared past his finish. Cody felt the cock swell and buck inside his ass. Hot cum splash against his guts. And Robert rammed his cock home as he sprayed into Cody's ass, plunging into him with all the strength of his body.

"I'm coming," Cody whispered. His body tightened, squeezing the cock that kept moving in his ass. "Patricia!"

"Come in me!" she commanded. She bucked her hips, making his cock slide against the slick walls of her pussy. "I want your come in my pussy!"

Six months of holding back exploded. Cody cried out as the strongest orgasm of his life pumped his balls dry. His wife's pussy grabbed at his cock, milking it as she writhed under him. His asshole flexed around Robert's cock, squeezing the last drops of cum out of it. Cody shuddered and shook, and when it was over, too soon, he collapsed into the arms of his wife.

He felt Robert's cock slip out of his ass. Felt the rivulet of come that followed it before he flexed tight. Cody rolled onto his back, panting. As his wife turned on her side in one direction, Robert stretched out on his other side. A long, deep look passed between the men.

Robert's lips found Cody's. Patricia moaned her appreciation as she began stroking her clit. Cody opened his mouth to take Robert's tongue, wrapping his arms around his new lover.

"Don't stop!" Patricia hissed. "Fuck! So fucking sexy!"

Cody had no intention of stopping. From the way Robert's mouth worked at his, neither did he. As soon as their lips would slip from the others, they would renew their passion. They were vaguely aware that Patricia had brought herself to yet another orgasm, but until she crawled into Cody's arms, they lost track of her.

"This was amazing," Robert said. He grinned at Cody before lifting his gaze to Patricia. "I'm so glad I let you talk me into this."

She lifted her mouth to kiss him, then lay her cheek on her husband's chest. Cody's cock was getting hard again. Her hand encouraged him, pumping slowly.

"I'm going to lock you up again," she told him. "You only get this when I want it. If I leave you two to your own devices, you'll never have enough come for me to enjoy."

Robert laughed, but Cody only smiled his agreement. If this was the life Patricia wanted, then who was he to deny it? And that was doubly true now that he understood it and wanted it, too.

"Don't laugh too much," she warned their boyfriend. "You're going to be locked up, too." She grinned. "When I have a stranger pounding my pussy for all he's worth, I don't want to be distracted by the thought that you're probably fucking my husband in the ass."

"Wait," Cody said, confused. "I thought that was just... training? Getting me ready for this?"

His wife shrugged.

"It was. But... I like it," she said. "Just because I'm getting two cocks exactly the way I like them doesn't mean I can't enjoy another cock once in a while." She gave her husband a wink. "Besides, you need to teach Robert how to lick my pussy clean after I've been pumped full of cum."

"No time like the present," Cody said.

Patricia agreed.

7

THERE WAS BARELY ENOUGH room for the two men to spoon against each other in the closet. Naked except for the matching chastity cages, Cody and Robert listened to Patricia fuck a stranger. Normally Cody was the little spoon with Robert, but he knew what it was like to hear to this the first time. He wanted to hold his boyfriend and comfort him.

"Yes," Patricia moaned. "Oh, yes."

"That's the biggest dick you've ever had, isn't it?" Patricia's response wasn't verbal, but it made the man laugh. "And you're going to take all of it. Every fucking inch."

Cody kissed the nape of Robert's neck. The man wrapped one of his hands around Cody's, where it lay against his chest. He pulled, and Cody hugged him tight. The bed began squeaking, something that it had started only recently.

"Fuck me! Fuck me!"

Robert turned in Cody's arms, slowly and careful not to make any sounds that would alert the man fucking Patricia. He pushed his face against Cody's chest, and Cody ran his fingers down Robert's back. He felt Robert's hand stroking his hip and thigh.

Outside, Patricia trilled through her first orgasm. The stranger laughed and began pumping harder. Every thrust was announced by his grunt of effort, the squeak of the bed, and Patricia's breath being forced from her lungs.

"That's it! Take it all!"

"Fuck me! Fuck me deep!"

Robert nuzzled under Cody's chin as Patricia and her lover devolved into animalistic sounds. Harder and faster, they fucked. Cody lowered his chin to kiss Robert's lips.

"It's okay," he dared to whisper, knowing his voice would never carry over the noise the two were making on the bed. "This is what she wants. For us."

"For all of us," Robert whispered back. "Do you ever get hard when you're in here?"

"I'm hard now," he chuckled softly.

"I want to fuck you. Hard."

Cody slid his tongue into his boyfriend's mouth. Sucked hard. Patricia was coming again, and the man showed no sign of slowing down.

"I want that, too," he whispered to Robert when he pulled his mouth away. "I want it, too."

He was reasonably sure he would get that, too. Patricia was fond of the three of them joining together. When she saw how much Robert needed it, she'd give it to him. Maybe, Cody thought, she'd finally have Robert in the middle, and he'd get to fuck Robert's ass.

Cody snuggled in Robert's arms. They shared a sigh, dreaming of each other with Patricia. And, as they waited, Patricia took everything she wanted from the stranger.

FemDomLit Sneak Peek

The Chastity Solution
By J.W. James

SARAH'S SHEETS WERE still damp, and her bedroom smelled like sex. But I was smart enough not to say anything as she pulled me into bed with her. Her naked skin was soft and warm against mine, and she felt right in my arms in a way no one else ever had.

"Just to be clear, we're doing this," she said, laying her head on my chest. "We're going to be... more than friends."

"As much as you'll let me have," I said, running my fingers through her hair.

Silence blanketed us. I felt her hand reach down until her fingers were able to trace the hard plastic encasing me. She kissed my chest before nuzzling into my throat. My cock throbbed to full life, making the cage bobble in Sarah's hand.

"Did you... ease your hunger?" she asked.

"No," I whispered. "If I can't be with you, then I want to be hungry for you."

Her fingers continued to trace the plastic cage.

"This is going to be permanent," she said, tapping it. "Not just a few weeks." She lifted up to look at me, her hand moving to brace against my chest. "I have to be honest, though. I have no plan to give up cock. And I don't mean unlocking you to service me."

I ran my hand up her back. There was a part of me that rebelled at the idea. That wanted to point out the injustice of keeping me caged where I couldn't even pleasure myself while she continued to screw other people. But it was only a part of me that hated it. And a small part at that.

"Am I allowed to ask for something in return for that freedom?" She shrugged and nodded. "When you're done with... whoever. Well, can I have this?"

"You want to hold me after I fuck someone else?"

"I do."

She slid up higher in the bed, her breasts now pushing against my chest. I turned towards her, my hand reaching for her hip. Her knee lifted just enough for mine to slip between her thighs. I pushed her hair behind her ear.

"I'm serious," she whispered. "I'm going to fuck other men in this bed while you wait for me to tell you that you're allowed to come cuddle me."

I swallowed.

"I know."

Don't miss out!

Visit the website below and you can sign up to receive emails whenever J.W. James publishes a new book. There's no charge and no obligation.

https://books2read.com/r/B-A-HRBLB-TLXKF

BOOKS 2 READ

Connecting independent readers to independent writers.

Also by J.W. James

Women Rule. Men Obey
Going Down on Her Lover
A Heart with Many Rooms

Watch for more at www.FemDomLitPublications.com/taboo.

About the Author

Welcome to the world of J.W. James, where the boundaries of desire are pushed to the limit and the power of women reigns supreme. As co-owner of FemDomLit Publications and Boss Beaver Publications, J.W. James is a masterful storyteller of exclusively woman-centered erotic romances and erotica.

The Visionary

J.W. James is a passionate advocate for relationships where women hold the reins of control and men are happy to obey. His writing is a testament to the beauty of submission, where the pleasure of the woman is the ultimate goal. With each carefully crafted sentence, J.W. James weaves a web of seduction, surrender, and unbridled passion.

The Author's Voice

J.W. James's writing style is a perfect blend of romance and eroticism, with a deep understanding of the intricacies of human desire. His words are laced with a sense of reverence, adoration, and submission, creating a world where women are worshipped and men are eager to please.

The Niche

J.W. James's work is centered around the themes of BDSM, cuckoldry, femdom, body worship/ownership, and pegging. His stories are designed to normalize relationships where women are in control, and men are happy to surrender to their desires.

The Promise

In J.W. James's world, you can expect to be transported to a place of unbridled passion, where the boundaries of desire are pushed to the limit. His writing is a promise of surrender, submission, and ultimate pleasure. So, come and immerse yourself in the world of J.W. James, where the power of women reigns supreme.

Get Ready to Surrender

Follow J.W. James on Twitter/X @ErosbyJWJames and stay updated on his latest releases, behind-the-scenes insights, and exclusive content. Be prepared to surrender to the pleasure of the woman, and discover a world where desire knows no bounds.

Read more at www.FemDomLitPublications.com/taboo.

About the Publisher

Welcome to FemdomLit Publications, where we redefine strength and surrender in the realm of erotic and romantic literature. Our mission is to illuminate the beauty and complexity of relationships where men find their satisfaction in yielding control to the women they choose to love. We believe that love transcends traditional roles, and that a man's ability to submit is not a sign of weakness, but a testament to his confidence, trust, and devotion.

Read more at www.femdomlitpublications.com.